I Thought I Saw an Alligator

by Beth Erlund

Let your imagination go wild!

B. Cer

Nov 2014

Erlund Johnson Studios

COLORADO ❖ FLORIDA

I wish to thank my husband **Dennis Johnson** for his endless support and patience as I embarked on this new adventure in my life. His artistic advice has proven to be invaluable.

Special thanks to **Carl Sams, Jean Stoick, Greg Dunn, John Gouin, Mort and Pati Fadum** for their countless hours of help in educating a rookie in the book industry. Their patience and creative advice made this book happen. Thanks also to **Jessica Egan** for editing, and my granddaughter **Krystal** for finding the *agillator* under my studio.

Inquires about this book and prints of the batiks should be addressed to:

Erlund Johnson Studios
22528 Blue Jay Rd.
Morrison, Colorado 80465
(303) 697-5188
www.erlundjohnsonstudios.com

Printed and bound in Canada by Friesens of Altona, Manitoba

Erlund, Beth
I Thought I Saw An Alligator / written by Beth Erlund
SUMMARY: A young child's mystery about what is hiding underneath the porch.
ISBN 0-9762306-0-5
Library of Congress Control Number: 2004097996

*For Dennis, Deb,
Cade, Jessica and
especially Krystal
whose imaginations
always give
me inspiration.*

I thought I saw an alligator
    underneath the backyard porch.

My mother said,
"Oh no, I don't
think it's an alligator,
probably just an armadillo
hiding under there."

My father said, "It can't be an alligator. I believe it's that pesky raccoon underneath the backyard porch."

My grandpa said,
"I believe that it's
not an alligator
but instead a big,
old leopard frog
trying to catch a
fly under there."

My brother said, "Aw, it's *not* an alligator. I bet you saw a stinky old skunk underneath the backyard porch."

My teacher said,
"I'm sure it's *not* an alligator,
probably a gopher tortoise
trying to stay cool
underneath the backyard porch."

My best friend Joe said,
"I can't believe it's an alligator.
I bet it's a very big
wolf spider that you
saw under there."

The mailman said,
  "I suspect it's *not* an alligator in
    this neighborhood. It's much more
      likely an opossum hiding under there."

My Aunt Ellen said, "I believe
it's *not* an alligator. You probably
spied a little evening bat
waiting for the night
underneath the backyard porch."

My grandma
said, "My dear,
I don't think it's
really an alligator.
 I would think
 you might have
seen a flying squirrel
  underneath the backyard porch."

My next-door neighbor said, "My feelings are that it's *not* an alligator. It's most likely a river otter playing hide-and-seek under there."

My little sister cried, "NO! NO!
There **IS** an *agillator* underneath the backyard porch.
I know there is! I see it there!"

All of a sudden,
    out popped a small green lizard from
        underneath the backyard porch.

A small green lizard who
thought he was
an alligator.

The End

An **ARMADILLO** is covered with hard, bony plates that protect it from its enemies.

Although **OPOSSUM** have a tail that can hold on to branches when climbing, only young ones are light enough to hang by their tails.

RACCOONS are very intelligent and have special adaptations that allow them to use their hands much like people do.

Growing up from little tadpoles, **LEOPARD FROGS** are well known for jumping very long distances.

Although **SKUNKS** have a bad smelling spray that they use when frightened, they are very helpful to people by eating many insects.

Although their mother has to teach them to swim, playful **RIVER OTTERS** can hold their breath under water for up to four minutes.

WOLF SPIDERS do not build a web but dig a hole in the ground. When they feel vibration of movement in the ground, they hide in the burrow waiting until danger passes.

FLYING SQUIRRELS do not really fly but glide from tree to tree. They use their tail to help direct their path and slow them down.

A **GOPHER TORTOISE** is known for digging long underground tunnels with sleeping areas at the very end.

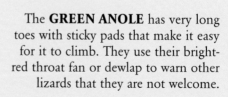

The **ALLIGATOR** is a reptile that lived during the era of dinosaurs. They often sneak up on their prey by looking like a floating log.

EVENING BATS fly at night, chasing insects for their dinner. You do not have to fear bats, they do not attack people.

The **GREEN ANOLE** has very long toes with sticky pads that make it easy for it to climb. They use their bright-red throat fan or dewlap to warn other lizards that they are not welcome.

batik: an art media using wax and dyes to make a picture on cloth. Over 2000 years ago, the Chinese used beeswax and resin to make designs to decorate fabrics that they dyed. Today, batik is created by drawing a pencil sketch on cloth and then proceeding to draw with hot beeswax and paraffin. The portions that are to remain white are drawn first, and then the lightest dye is applied.